THE HORRIBLE

AND THE GOLDEN MAIDEN

by Dik Browne

Volume III of
THE BEST OF HAGAR THE HORRIBLE

TOR

A TOM DOHERTY ASSOCIATES BOOK

HAGAR THE HORRIBLE AND THE GOLDEN MAIDEN

Hagar the Horrible and the Golden Maiden is a selection of cartoons taken from The Best of Hagar the Horrible, originally published by Simon and Schuster in May 1981.

A TOR Book
Published by Tom Doherty Associates, Inc.
49 West 24 Street
New York, NY 10010

ISBN: 0-812-50560-3   Can. ISBN: 0-812-50561-1

Second printing: September 1989

Printed in the United States of America

0 9 8 7 6 5 4 3 2

A NIGHT OUT

BACKTALK

HEALTH NUT

THE TANTRUM

WEIRD WELL

NAG NAG NAG

WHO, ME?

VIKING VERSE

GETS WORSE
AND WORSE!

WHO WOULD WASTE
A DAY LIKE THIS
FULL OF SUNSHINE
FULL OF BLISS

SHALL I SPEND IT WITH A FROG
TRADING WISDOM IN A BOG

THE TASTER!

INTRODUCTIONS

INSPIRATION!

DOG GONE

CAMPING OUT

VIKING STYLE

MESSENGER

REVENGER!

THE OPTIMIST

THE CASTLE

REMEMBER WHAT I TOLD YOU— STICK WITH ME AND SOMEDAY YOU'LL BE SITTING PRETTY!

I CAN'T BELIEVE IT!

YOU CAN BELIEVE IT! IT TOOK A LOT, BUT—

BARGAINS

MANNERS!

SCIENCE

STOUT HEAR[T]

& WEAK KNEES

LANDFALL

TIPS FOR

WHAT A PLACE TO INVADE! IT DOESN'T EVEN HAVE PEOPLE!

THIS YOUR FIRST TIME IN SIBERIA? YOU OUGHTA TAKE IN THE SIGHTS.

A TOURIST

TIME OUT!

THE DOOR

GOURMETS